My dearest puppy, Storm,

I hope this letter reaches you safe and sound. You have been so brave since you had to flee from the evil wolf Shadow.

Do not worry about me. I will hide here until you are strong enough to return and lead our pack. For now you must move on – you must hide from Shadow and his spies. If Shadow finds this letter I believe he will try to destroy it . . .

Find a good friend – someone to help finish my message to you. Because what I have to say to you is important. What I have to say is this: you must always

Please don't feel lonely. Trust in your friends and all will be well.

Your loving mother,

Canista

Sue Bentley's books for children often include animals, fairies and wildlife. She lives in Northampton and enjoys reading, going to the cinema, relaxing by her garden pond and watching the birds feeding their babies on the lawn. At school she was always getting told off for daydreaming or staring out of the window – but she now realizes that she was storing up ideas for when she became a writer. She has met and owned many cats and dogs and each one has brought a special kind of magic to her life.

Sue Bentley

Magic Puppy

Snowy Wishes

Illustrated by Angela Swan

PUFFIN

To Teddy – tiny dog with a big heart

PUFFIN BOOKS

Published by the Penguin Group
Penguin Books Ltd, 80 Strand, London WC2R ORL, England
Penguin Group (USA) Inc., 375 Hudson Street, New York, New York 10014, USA
Penguin Group (Canada), 90 Eglinton Avenue East, Suite 700, Toronto, Ontario, Canada M4P 2Y3
(a division of Pearson Penguin Canada Inc.)
Penguin Ireland, 25 St Stephen's Green, Dublin 2, Ireland (a division of Penguin Books Ltd)
Penguin Group (Australia), 250 Camberwell Road, Camberwell, Victoria 3124, Australia
(a division of Pearson Australia Group Pty Ltd)
Penguin Books India Pvt Ltd, 11 Community Centre, Panchsheel Park, New Delhi – 110 017, India
Penguin Group (NZ), 67 Apollo Drive, Rosedale, North Shore 0632, New Zealand
(a division of Pearson New Zealand Ltd)
Penguin Books (South Africa) (Pty) Ltd, 24 Sturdee Avenue, Rosebank,
Johannesburg 2196, South Africa

Penguin Books Ltd, Registered Offices: 80 Strand, London WC2R ORL, England

puffinbooks.com

First published 2008
010

Text copyright © Sue Bentley, 2008
Illustrations copyright © Angela Swan, 2008
All rights reserved

The moral right of the author and illustrator has been asserted

Set in Bembo
Typeset by Palimpsest Book Production Limited,
Grangemouth, Stirlingshire
Made and printed in England by Clays Ltd, St Ives plc

British Library Cataloguing in Publication Data
A CIP catalogue record for this book is available from the British Library

ISBN: 978-0-141-32383-1

www.greenpenguin.co.uk

Penguin Books is committed to a sustainable
future for our business, our readers and our planet.
This book is made from Forest Stewardship
Council™ certified paper.

Prologue

Storm rolled on his back on the stony ground. The young silver-grey wolf enjoyed the scratchy feeling against his thick fur. It felt good to be back in his homeland.

Suddenly, a fierce howl rose into the air and echoed over the quiet hillside.

'Shadow!' gasped Storm. The fierce lone wolf who had attacked Storm's

Moon-claw pack was very close. He should have known that it wasn't safe to return.

There was a flash of bright gold light and a silent explosion of gold sparks. The young wolf disappeared and in its place stood a tiny fluffy white Labrador puppy with floppy ears and big midnight-blue eyes.

Storm's short puppy legs trembled. He needed to find somewhere to hide, and quickly.

Halfway up the slope, thick bushes clung to the rough ground. Storm raced towards them, his little paws kicking up spurts of dust. A dark wolf shape was crouching near one of the bushes. Storm's breath caught in his throat with terror and he skidded sideways in an attempt to escape.

'In here, my son,' the wolf called in a deep gentle growl.

'Mother!' Storm yapped with relief.

He stopped and raced back towards the bush where she was hiding. As he reached her, Storm's whole body wriggled and his silky little tail wagged delightedly.

Canista reached out a huge paw and gathered her disguised cub close against her warm body. She licked Storm's fluffy white muzzle. 'I am glad to see you again, but you cannot stay. Shadow is looking for you. He wants to lead the Moon-claw pack, but the others will not follow him while you live.'

Storm's midnight-blue eyes sparked

with anger and fear. 'He has already killed my father and litter brothers and wounded you. I will fight Shadow and make him leave our lands.'

Canista showed her strong sharp teeth in a proud smile. 'Bravely said, but Shadow is too strong for you and I am still weak from his poisoned bite and cannot help you. Go back to the other world. Hide there and return when you are wiser and your magic is stronger.'

Storm whined softly. He knew his mother was right, but he hated to leave her.

He huffed out a warm puppy breath that glittered with a thousand tiny gold sparks. The healing mist swirled round Canista's paw and then sank into her thick grey fur.

'Thank you, Storm. The pain is much better,' she rumbled softly.

Suddenly, another terrifying howl rang out and there came the sound of enormous paws thudding up the slope towards them.

'I know you are there, Storm. Let us finish this!' growled a harsh cruel voice.

'Go now! Save yourself!' Canista urged.

Storm whimpered as he felt the power gathering inside his tiny form. Bright gold sparks ignited in his fluffy white fur. A bright gold light spread around him. And grew brighter . . .

Chapter
ONE

'Robyn, love. Are you awake?'

At the sound of her mum's voice in the doorway, Robyn Parsons sat up slowly. Her bunk was moving very slightly with the motion of the ship. From somewhere deep below her she could hear the faint rumbling of the *Sea Princess*'s enormous engines.

'I wasn't asleep. I was just resting,'

Robyn murmured. 'Uh-oh,' she breathed as her tummy gave a familiar lurch.

'Still feeling weak and wobbly?' Mrs Parsons said gently. 'Poor old you. That's nearly two days you've been stuck in here.'

'I know,' Robyn said glumly, feeling very down in the dumps.

She'd been looking forward to this Christmas even more than usual.

Robyn didn't have any brothers or
sisters and her dad worked away from
home a lot. This was the first chance
for ages to spend lots of time with
him and they would be all together as
a family.

'I think we deserve a holiday with
guaranteed snow, fairy lights and lots of
atmosphere! Leave it to me,' Mr Parsons
had declared.

And now here they all were, all
aboard the *Sea Princess* for a winter
cruise round the wild and beautiful
coast of Norway.

Robyn sighed. At this rate, she was
going to be lucky if she caught a
glimpse of any snow-capped mountains
through the cabin window, let alone
spend any time with her dad. It looked

like this was going to be another lonely
Christmas after all.

'How come you and Dad are OK?
I can barely even stand up without
wanting to be sick,' she grumbled.

'It's just sheer bad luck,' her mum
said sympathetically. 'We had no idea
that you'd react so badly to a sea

voyage or we'd have chosen a different way of spending Christmas.' She handed Robyn a glass. 'Have a drink of water. It might help.'

Robyn sipped the water. She felt a tiny bit better after having a drink. 'Thanks, Mum. I think I might stay sitting up. Maybe I'll look through that music magazine you got me. Where's Dad?'

'In the sun lounge, reading his paper. Are you sure you wouldn't like me to bring you something? Maybe a sandwich or some fruit?'

At the thought of food, Robyn pulled a face. 'I couldn't eat a thing.'

Mrs Parsons shook her head slowly. 'I'm really starting to wonder whether we shouldn't get off the ship at the next port and arrange to take you home.'

'No! You can't!' Robyn said at once and then wished that she hadn't spoken so loudly. Her head felt as if it was spinning. 'Dad will be so disappointed if we waste this holiday. And you've been really looking forward to it for ages.'

'So have you, love,' her mum reminded her gently. 'This was supposed to be a really special Christmas together, remember?'

Robyn nodded. 'I know, but we'll have lots more of them,' she said, trying hard to hide her disappointment for her mum's sake. 'I don't see why you and Dad can't still have a good time. I'll be fine in here by myself. I'm nearly ten years old, aren't I? And I *have* to start feeling better soon. No one stays seasick forever!'

Mrs Parsons shook her head slowly. 'I'm still not happy about leaving you alone. I'm just going to pop back to have a word with your dad. Let's see what he has to say about this. I won't be long.'

Robyn's shoulders slumped as the cabin door closed. Even though it wasn't her fault that she felt so ill, she knew she'd feel really guilty if their cruise was cut short.

'It's just not fair! I'm so fed up of being sick!' she grumbled to herself.

She took a deep breath and decided to get up. Maybe her mum and dad would change their minds about taking her home if she could convince them that she was feeling stronger.

Pushing back her quilt, Robyn slowly swung her legs over the side of her bunk. Her head swam a bit, but she stood up determinedly and reached for her jeans and fleece top. She was a bit wobbly on her feet, but she took her time getting dressed and finally managed it OK.

'I'm much better. I'm fine,' she told herself determinedly as she bent down to pull on her trainers. Suddenly, a strong dizzy feeling washed over her and she lost her balance.

'Oh,' Robyn gasped, toppling forward.

She threw out her arms, ready for a painful bruising landing, when a brilliant golden flash and a shower of sparks lit up the small cabin. Time seemed to stand still and a warm

tingling sensation ran down Robyn's spine. She felt a sudden jolt, but there was no hard landing.

To her complete astonishment Robyn found herself sprawled full length on her tummy on a sort of bouncy raft, made of shimmering gold-coloured bubbles, and whizzing all around her was an ice-storm of spinning glittering sparks.

Robyn caught her breath as she felt herself slowly rising up into a sitting position and then being lowered gently on to the floor. The bubble raft and sparks dissolved with a loud crackling noise, like crisp wrappers being crumpled up.

Robyn sat there shakily on the floor and looked around nervously.

What had just happened? She felt like pinching herself to see if she had been dreaming.

'I hope you are not hurt,' woofed a strange little voice.

Robyn nearly jumped out of her skin. 'Who said that?' She twisted round, her eyes searching the small cabin.

Crouching on top of the neat chest of drawers opposite, Robyn saw a tiny fluffy white puppy, with cute floppy ears, a silky white tail and midnight-blue eyes. Thousands of tiny diamond-bright golden sparkles glittered in its thick fur.

Chapter
TWO

Robyn's eyes widened. Her mum must
have brought the cute toy in to cheer
her up and then forgotten to tell her
about it. She must be more affected by
her seasickness than she'd realized – first
she'd imagined floating on a sparkly
bubble raft and now she thought she'd
heard this toy puppy speak to her!

Robyn stood up and went to reach

out towards the toy. 'Hello. Aren't you
gorgeous? I wonder where Mum
found you.'

'I came here by myself,' the puppy
woofed. 'When you fell I used my
magic to stop you being hurt. I am
sorry if I startled you.'

Robyn gasped and pulled her hand
back as if it had been burned. 'You . . .
you *can* talk!' she cried.

The puppy blinked up at her with
wide midnight-blue eyes. Despite its
tiny size it didn't seem to be afraid of

her. 'Yes. I am Storm of the Moon-claw pack. What is your name? And what is this strange moving place?'

'Robyn. Robyn Parsons. And we're on a ship called *Sea Princess*. I'm here on a Christmas cruise with my parents,' Robyn explained, her mind still whirling. She found it difficult to take all this in, but she didn't want to scare the amazing puppy away. 'Um . . . I don't know what you did just now, but thanks for helping me. I could have hurt myself badly.'

'You are welcome,' Storm yapped.

Robyn slowly backed up to the edge of her bunk and then sat down. 'Sorry, I'm feeling a bit sick. I've been like this since we came on board.'

Storm's little pointed face clouded with concern. 'I will make you better.'

Robyn instantly felt another warm
tingling sensation down her back as
Storm reached out one little fluffy
white paw and sent a fountain of tiny
sparks towards her. They whirled round
her, humming like tiny worker bees
before disappearing. She felt the sickness
washing downwards and draining out of
her toes, just as if she'd been standing
under the flow of a warm shower.

'Wow! That's amazing,' she cried
delightedly, jumping up. 'I don't feel
sick any more and I'm not dizzy or
anything! Thanks again, Storm!'

'That is good.' Storm grinned,
showing his sharp little teeth, and then
his face took on a serious expression.
'I need to hide now, Robyn. Can you
help me?'

'I'd love to, but why do you need to do that?' Robyn asked, looking down at the cute white puppy who was beginning to tremble all over.

Storm's midnight-blue eyes darkened with anger. 'An evil lone wolf attacked our Moon-claw pack – he is called Shadow. Shadow killed my father and litter brothers and wounded my mother. He wants to lead our pack, but the others are waiting for me.'

'But how can you lead a wolf pack? You're a tiny pu–' Robyn began.

'Stand back, please!' Storm interrupted.

There was a dazzling flare of golden light, which blinded Robyn for a moment. For a second or two she couldn't see anything. But when her

sight cleared the cute white puppy
had gone and in its place a
magnificent young silver-grey wolf
stood proudly, almost filling the whole
of the tiny cabin. Its thick neck-ruff
glittered all over as if it had been
dipped in gold dust.

Robyn caught her breath and would
have backed away if there had been
room. 'Storm?' she gasped, eyeing the

young wolf's sharp teeth, strong muscles and huge powerful paws.

'Yes, it is me. Do not be afraid. I will not harm you,' Storm replied in a deep velvety growl.

Robyn had hardly got used to the great majestic wolf, when there was a final flash of dazzling light. A shower of bright sparks crackled harmlessly down around her and Storm reappeared as a cute fluffy white puppy.

'Wow! You really are a wolf! That's an amazing disguise,' Robyn whispered.

Storm tucked his little white tail between his legs and Robyn saw that he was beginning to tremble again. 'Shadow will recognize me if he finds out I'm here and then he will use his magic against me. Please will you help?'

Robyn's soft heart went out to the tiny scared puppy. She bent down and stroked his soft little head. Storm was impressive as his real self, but in his cute puppy disguise he was totally adorable.

'Of course I'll help you and –' Robyn stopped as she realized something. 'Oh, I don't think animals are allowed on board. I could try to hide you in my cabin, but it's only small and you'll be really bored if you have to stay in there for the whole time.'

'I can come everywhere with you. I will use my magic so that only you can see and hear me,' Storm woofed eagerly. A couple of tiny sparks danced round his floppy white ears and then blinked out. 'It is done.'

'You've made yourself invisible?
Cool!' Robyn said delightedly. She
picked Storm up and gave him a
cuddle. His white fur was thick and
silky and smelled of cold fresh air.
'Let's go and explore *Sea Princess*
together!'

'I would like that!' Storm's little white muzzle wrinkled in a smile and he licked her chin with his pink tongue.

'I can't wait to go and find Mum and Dad and tell them about you.' Robyn smiled down at him.

'No!' Storm's face was suddenly serious. 'You can never tell anyone my secret. Promise me,' he woofed gently.

Robyn felt disappointed that she couldn't share the news about her wonderful new friend with her parents – she was sure they would love him too. But if it would help to keep the tiny puppy safe, Robyn decided to keep this secret to herself.

'OK. I won't say anything. Cross my heart.'

'What's this promise you're making?'
said Mr Parsons, coming into the cabin.

'Dad!' Robyn whirled round in shock
to see her mum and dad standing there.
She'd been so busy talking to Storm
that she hadn't heard the cabin door
open. 'I was just promising . . . erm . . .
myself,' she said, thinking quickly. 'That
I was . . . um . . . going to have the

best time ever, now that I feel better. Because I've got lots of time to make up, haven't I?'

'You certainly have,' her dad said, looking surprised but delighted. 'Well, I must say that you seem to have made a miracle recovery. And there your mum was, wondering whether we ought to take you home!'

Robyn still couldn't quite believe that her mum and dad hadn't noticed Storm in her arms. But when neither of them said anything about the tiny puppy, she felt herself starting to relax.

'No one's going home. So there!' Robyn exclaimed, her eyes shining.

She spun round and pretended to straighten her duvet, giving Storm the chance to jump on to her bunk.

When Robyn turned back to her parents, her mum was beaming at her. 'I can hardly believe it. You're like a totally different girl to the one I was talking to just a few minutes ago. It's just like magic!'

If only Mum knew how right she was, Robyn thought, smiling inwardly.

'Well, you look ready to leave the cabin at last. I expect you'd like a look around to see what you've been missing. Where do you fancy going?' her dad asked.

Robyn's tummy rumbled and she realized that she was starving.

'Lunch it is, then!' said her mum.

As Robyn followed her parents to an upper deck, Storm trotted invisibly at her heel. Robyn had a warm glow

inside. After a false start, her holiday
was just beginning and she now had
a wonderful new friend to share it
with too.

Chapter
THREE

'Doesn't everywhere look great?' Robyn
said to Storm. 'It makes me feel all
Christmassy.'

They were walking across a part of
the ship with a domed ceiling and large
picture windows, swathed with
evergreen garlands. Lanterns and
traditional decorations made of wood
and tin were strung around the walls

and Christmas trees in pots gleamed
with hundreds of fairy lights.

Robyn peered through one of the
large windows. The Norwegian sky was
filled with a strange dark-grey light and
the heavy rolling sea looked like a sheet
of ridged silver.

'It's really weird to think that it never
gets completely light during the day in
winter. I don't know if I'd like to live
here all year round,' she whispered to
Storm. 'But it looks amazing, doesn't it?
Like something out of a fairy story. You
can just imagine scaly monsters in the

sea and fierce trolls and frost giants living in the mountains.'

'Trolls and frost giants?' Storm flattened his ears and his silky white tail drooped.

Robyn grinned. 'Sorry. I didn't mean to scare you. I read up about Viking legends and stuff when I knew we were coming here on holiday.'

Storm still seemed unsure about being on board a ship. He reared up on to his back legs beside her and pressed his little nose to the window. His big midnight-blue eyes widened and he gave a worried little whine.

'Are you OK?' Robyn asked, wishing she hadn't mentioned giants and trolls now. She hadn't realized that Storm would take her seriously.

'I think we are lost,' Storm woofed. 'There is so much grey water and sky, but I cannot see any land.'

'That's because we're looking out on to open sea on this side,' Robyn explained. 'We can go up on deck, if you like, and then you'll be able to see land and mountains.'

Storm nodded, still not looking entirely happy as he jumped back down.

Robyn didn't expect that any of the magical wolves from the Moon-claw pack had ever been on a cruise ship; or on any other kind of ship for that matter. In his home world, Storm was a land animal. No wonder he was ill at ease.

'Come on, let's catch up with Mum

34

and Dad,' she said to Storm, changing the subject. 'I could eat a horse!'

Storm's face showed surprise. 'A horse? I have seen one of those. It is very large!'

'I know. I wouldn't really want to eat one. It's just something that people say when they're really hungry!'

Storm's little white muzzle twitched
in a grin. Robyn was pleased to see
that his anxious look had completely
disappeared.

'I am very hungry too!' he yapped,
falling into step with Robyn as she set
off again.

A buzz of conversation and a riot of
delicious smells greeted them as they
entered the restaurant. Robyn could see
her mum and dad beginning to help
themselves from the food service area.
She picked up a tray and joined them.

'Wow! Look at all this!' she whispered
to Storm, her mouth watering. 'I hardly
know what to choose.'

There was an enormous display of
food with hot and cold dishes of all
kinds, salads, sandwiches, puddings, cakes

and baskets of fruit and chocolates. In the centre there was an entire miniature village made of iced gingerbread and an amazing ice sculpture of a polar bear.

Robyn heaped her plate with food for her and Storm, and then followed her mum and dad to an empty table. As soon as she sat down Storm jumped up on to her lap and curled up.

After almost two days of just drinking water, Robyn ate hungrily. She slipped bits of meat and fish under the table to Storm without her mum and dad noticing.

'Human food tastes very good,' Storm woofed, licking his chops when he'd finished. 'Thank you, Robyn.'

Robyn's mum and dad were wondering what to do next. 'We could

go swimming or watch a film or even
have a sauna,' her mum said. 'There's a
games room, shops, an Internet cafe and
loads of organized events too.'

'Could we go up on deck and look
at the view?' Robyn asked. If Storm
could see that they weren't far from
land, he might feel less nervous about
being on *Sea Princess.*

'Fine by me,' her mum said. 'I think
we should be steaming through a fjord
by now. It should be quite spectacular.'

Up on deck a cold wind was blowing
and Robyn wrapped her coat round
Storm to keep him warm. The tiny
puppy was peeping out from the front
opening and Robyn could feel him
snuggled against her chest, like a fluffy
hot water bottle.

Sea Princess was moving up a wide channel that had been created thousands of years ago by melting glaciers. The fjord stretched deep into the surrounding mountains. Painted wooden houses were clustered on the slopes and the towering, snow-capped tops were hidden by clouds.

Some people sat on deck in chairs, bundled up in warm blankets as they enjoyed the dramatic scenery. Others were lining the ship's rail, pointing out details to each other and taking photographs.

Robyn found a place to stand at the rail and looked down at the grey-green water, far below. 'I wonder how deep it is here,' she commented to Storm.

'Some of these fjords are twelve

hundred metres deep,' her dad said, coming to stand beside her. 'That's as deep as the mountains you can see.'

Robyn realized that she must have spoken more loudly than she'd intended to and her dad had thought she was speaking to him. She would have to be more careful about keeping Storm's secret.

'That's scarily deep,' she said to her dad.

Some way further on, the ship slowly rounded a bend and Robyn saw a waterfall gushing from a gorge in a high cliff. Jagged icicles, like spears, hung down from the rock and the foaming curtain of water fell straight down between them.

'Warm enough, love?' her dad asked

cheerfully. 'This icy air's really bringing
the roses back to your cheeks.'

'I feel fine. I don't mind the cold that
much,' Robyn said, giving her dad a
hug. Storm gave a little warning squeak
as he got a bit squashed between the
two of them. 'Sorry!' Robyn whispered
to him, when her dad broke away.

'Well, I've had enough of it for now,'

her mum said with a shiver. 'I think I might have a sauna to warm me up.'

'That's a good idea. I'll come with you. What about you, Robyn?' her dad asked.

Robyn shook her head. 'No thanks.' She didn't fancy all that hot steam and she didn't want to leave Storm by himself. 'I think I'll stay out here for a while. I'll come and meet you at the health suite.'

'All right, love,' her mum said. 'By the way, the ship's docking at a fairly big town this afternoon. I thought we could all go ashore and do some shopping.'

'Sounds great. Enjoy your sauna. See you later,' Robyn called as her parents walked away. Now that she felt well

enough to spend some time with her
mum and dad, she definitely didn't mind
wandering round by herself with Storm.

Her dad looked over his shoulder and
winked at her. 'Watch out for trolls.'

Robyn grinned. 'I will!'

She didn't notice Storm shrinking
further down inside her coat, his dewy
eyes looking round nervously.

The fjord began to get narrower and
more winding. The sides of the
mountains were steeper here, without
any houses or farms. Ice and snow
clung to the jagged black rock face and
the grey clouds seemed lower.

Robyn was quite enjoying the
gloomy landscape. It was easy to believe
that fierce trolls lay in wait for unwary
travellers.

Suddenly, a bloodcurdling cry rang out behind her. Robyn almost jumped out of her skin and Storm yelped in terror. Robyn whipped round to see a number of hairy men with huge teeth, pointed ears and lumpy faces running towards her across the deck. They were dressed in rough fur cloaks and shaking their fists.

'Trolls!' gasped Robyn.

Storm growled, his whole body tensing inside Robyn's coat.

Robyn's heart beat fast. Some of the other passengers screamed and one little girl hid behind her dad.

And then Robyn saw one of the 'trolls' adjusting his mask and another one of them straightening his hairy wig. It was just some of the ship's crew who had dressed up to put on a special performance for the passengers.

She started to laugh. 'It's OK, Storm. It's only . . .' she began, in a reassuring voice, but it was too late.

Robyn felt a familiar warm prickling sensation down her spine as big gold sparks flowered in Storm's fluffy white fur and his ears crackled with magical power.

Something very strange was about to happen.

Chapter
FOUR

Robyn watched in complete amazement as Storm leapt out of her coat and sprang on to the deck, trailing a comet's tail of gold sparks.

He lifted one tiny front paw and sent a huge spray of glittering sparks whooshing into the icy air. Robyn saw them hang there for a second and then transform into greyish smoke, which sank down on to the trolls in the thickest mist she had ever seen.

'Hey! What's going on?' one of them cried from the middle of the dense mist.

'Oops, sorry,' said another one, as he tripped over his friend.

They couldn't see where they were going. Robyn could hear the disguised crew members staggering about and bashing into each other. The other passengers thought it was all part of the

act and began laughing and cheering them on.

But as the magical mist spread, they became swallowed up in it too.

'Follow me, Robyn! I will save you from the monsters,' Storm yapped. His little form glowed as brightly as a lantern as he scampered towards the door to the lower deck.

'Come back, Storm!' Robyn called to him above all the noise. 'They're not real trolls. They're people dressed up. It's just for fun!'

Storm stopped dead and then padded back towards her. In the little pool of light made by his magically glowing body, Robyn could see a shamefaced expression creep over his fluffy white face.

'I am sorry. I thought that you were in danger,' Storm yapped quietly, flattening his ears.

'It's OK. I know you were only trying to protect me, but I think you'd better make the fog disappear now,' she said gently.

Storm nodded.

He sent a big spurt of bright gold sparks whooshing across the deck. The sparkles were like a powerful jet spray at a car wash, magically blasting the fog into thin strands. Seconds later it all blew away on the icy wind.

The disguised crewmen stood there on the clear deck, looking puzzled. Their wigs were all crooked and their troll masks were dangling round their necks. But they soon recovered.

Straightening their costumes, they
skipped round the deck, roaring and
waving their arms.

Delighted applause broke out as
more of the crew came on to the
deck, holding trays of hot drinks, food
and snacks.

'You must pay the price for entering
our land,' one of the trolls boomed,
grinning broadly. 'We order you to
feast with us on troll brew and hot
troll soup!'

As everyone began helping
themselves, Robyn decided that this
was a good time for her and Storm to
make their exit.

Later that afternoon after *Sea Princess*
docked at the harbour, Robyn, Storm

and her mum and dad went ashore.
They caught a bus to the south of the
city with lots of other people on the
cruise.

Robyn sat with Storm safely inside
the shoulder bag on her lap. He stuck
his head out to look at the broad
snow-covered streets and modern shops
and offices.

Robyn could see coloured lights
gleaming from house windows and
there were lots of green wreaths hung

on doors. Here and there, they passed
traditional wooden buildings, painted in
shades of red, orange or mustard.

'Everything looks so Christmassy here.
I love it,' she whispered. 'I hope I can
get some presents for Mum and Dad.'

Storm twisted round and looked up
at her. 'What is Christmas?'

'Oh, of course. I don't suppose you
have it in your world, do you?' Robyn
realized. 'Christmas is a special time
when we celebrate the baby Jesus being
born. We sing carols and families all get
together and exchange presents and eat
lots of yummy food. Dad usually stuffs
himself with turkey, mince pies and
cake and then moans about his trousers
being tight! At least, that's what we
usually do at home. It's going to seem

a bit different this year. We celebrate Christmas on Christmas Eve aboard *Sea Princess*.'

Storm looked a bit puzzled but his midnight-blue eyes were twinkling with excitement. 'It sounds very odd, but I think I will enjoy Christmas, especially the food!'

The bus stopped near an enormous cathedral with a towering spire and lots of amazing stone carving. Coloured light streamed out on to the snow from its stained-glass windows.

Robyn's mum produced a tourist brochure she'd picked up on the way to the bus. 'I think I'd like to look around inside that cathedral. It says here that it's getting on for a thousand years old. Imagine that!' she said enthusiastically.

'Wow!' Robyn said. She couldn't imagine anything being that old. But she didn't really fancy walking round some musty-smelling old cathedral for hours, however impressive it was. 'Do we all have to go?' she asked, without enthusiasm.

Mr Parsons smiled. 'I don't think so. I'm not as interested in old buildings as your mum. You and I'll go shopping and meet her later.'

'Oh good,' Robyn said, relieved.

'Fine,' Mrs Parsons said. 'I'm quite happy to mooch about by myself.' She turned to her husband. 'I'll see you back here in a couple of hours?'

Mr Parsons nodded. 'Sounds good.'

Robyn waved to her mum as she set off towards the cathedral and then she and her dad set off in search of interesting shops. Storm leaned up and hooked his front paws over her shoulder bag, so that he could look at the surroundings.

They had been walking for a couple of minutes when Storm reached out and tapped Robyn's arm with one front paw. She looked down to see that he'd pricked up his little ears.

'I can hear music,' he yapped.

'I can too,' Robyn whispered. 'Can you hear that, Dad?' she said in a louder voice. 'It's coming from over there.'

Mr Parsons listened. 'Oh yes. It's quite faint, but it sounds like folk music. Let's go and have a look.'

As they walked to the end of the street, the music got louder. They reached a cobbled square, surrounded by stalls, heaped with crystallized fruit, gingerbread and spiced biscuits. Cheery lanterns were strung between the buildings encircling the small square, and green garlands and decorations were looped between the stalls.

Storm yipped excitedly as he saw the bandstand, with musicians playing violins. Women in colourful felt skirts and men in waistcoats and buckled shoes were dancing. A festive smell of spiced wine and roasted nuts filled the frosty air.

'Oh, it's a Christmas festival!' Robyn exclaimed delightedly.

Chapter
FIVE

Robyn sipped a cup of hot spiced apple juice as she watched some children building snowmen. It was a competition and a number of half-built snow trolls and elves stood in one corner of the square. There was even a Father Christmas snowman with his snow reindeer.

In the strange half-light, the glowing

lanterns cast a cheerful glow over everything. Storm jumped out of Robyn's bag in another little flurry of sparks.

At first, Robyn was worried that his little paws would get cold on the frozen ground. But Storm's white ears sizzled with tiny sparks and she noticed that he was now wearing four tiny furry boots.

He looked so cute wearing them that Robyn burst out laughing, which

she quickly turned into a cough. She didn't want to hurt her puppy friend's feelings.

As she and her dad wandered around the market stalls, they bought cheese, chocolate and spice cakes for presents to take home for Gran and Gramps. Robyn didn't see anything she wanted to buy for her mum and dad.

She spotted a shop a few metres away on the other side of the square. 'I'm just going to pop into that shop over there. I won't be long,' she told her dad.

Mr Parsons nodded. 'All right. I'll still be here.'

Storm scampered after Robyn as she headed across the square. Inside the shop it felt really warm after the cold outside. Robyn took off her hat and gloves and stuffed them in her coat pocket.

There were lots of people looking at the gifts and cuddly toys. Robyn noticed a rack of knitwear. Maybe her mum would like a traditional hand-knitted cardigan.

As she went to have a closer look, Robyn heard raised voices. A sales assistant was speaking sharply to a tall slim girl with black hair, who looked about twelve years old.

'I am not a thief!' the girl said in a low angry voice. She was wearing a red felt skirt, decorated with bands of embroidery and sturdy leather boots.

'We'll see about that!' the sales assistant shouted, beckoning to a man from another counter.

As Robyn stood at the far end of the long clothes rack, the man hurried over. 'What's the problem?' he asked the assistant.

'This young lady has taken an expensive *lusekofte*. See, there is the empty hanger,' the woman said crossly, pointing to the rack of knitted cardigans. 'I demand that she opens her bag so that I can search it!'

'Did you see her take it?' the man asked.

The woman put her hands on her hips. 'No. But she must have. One's missing and it was there a minute ago!'

'I told you. I have not taken it. I would never do that,' the girl said calmly, clutching her bag with two hands.

Her face was pale, expect for her
cheeks, which were flushed a deep red.
Robyn could see that the girl looked
close to tears and admired the way she

was sticking up for herself against the
bossy assistant.

'That woman's determined to search
the girl's bag. I hope she hasn't pinched
anything,' Robyn whispered to Storm.

Suddenly, Storm's head came up and
he gave a triumphant woof.

Diving beneath the rack of cardigans,
the tiny puppy jumped up and ferreted
about. He grabbed something and a
loose cardigan came free. Storm
dropped it on to the floor before
padding back to Robyn.

'Oh, well done, Storm!' Robyn
praised him, pleased that it looked like
the young girl hadn't taken anything.
'The cardigan must have slipped off its
hanger. It was lucky you spotted a bit
of its dangling sleeve, Storm.' The sales

assistant obviously hadn't looked carefully enough.

On impulse, Robyn picked up the empty hanger and stepped forward. 'Excuse me,' she said politely, holding it up. 'Are you looking for the cardigan that was on this?'

The two assistants and the dark-haired girl turned to look at her.

'I know where it is,' the woman snapped. 'It's inside this young person's bag!'

'Are you sure?' Robyn asked. 'Because there's one on the floor. Look.'

The assistant frowned and went to investigate. A deep flush crept up her face as she came back holding the cardigan. 'I . . . er . . . seem to have made a mistake. We'll say no more about it,' she said shortly. Snatching the empty hanger from Robyn, she marched briskly away.

The male assistant threw the girl an apologetic look and then hurried back to his counter.

Robyn's eyes widened. 'What a rotten cheek! That woman didn't even say sorry!'

'It does not matter,' the girl replied,

shrugging. 'I knew I had done nothing, but thank you for speaking up for me. I am Kristiana Magga. Everyone calls me Krista. What is your name?'

'Robyn. Robyn Parsons. I'm here on holiday with my mum and dad,' Robyn said, surprised that the girl was so calm after the unpleasant scene. She saw that Krista had high cheekbones and unusual dark eyes, which were slightly tilted at the corners.

'I am very glad to meet you,' Krista said with a wide smile.

'Me too,' Robyn said. 'Do you live here?'

Krista shook her head. 'I am visiting friends. My Uncle Nikolai and Aunt Jorun are with me. Oh, here they are now.'

A man and woman came towards them. Robyn saw that they had high cheekbones and dark hair, like Krista. Krista's aunt also wore a blue felt skirt and strong leather boots. There was a fringed gold shawl round her shoulders, pinned with a circular brooch.

'This is my new friend Robyn,' Krista said.

Robyn glowed at Krista's description of her as a friend. Since they'd only just met, it was a lovely thing to do.

Krista then told her aunt and uncle about the sales assistant who had accused her of stealing. '. . . and Robyn proved that I didn't steal it after she found the *lusekofte* on the floor,' she finished.

It wasn't me, actually, it was Storm,

Robyn thought, wishing that she could tell them all how brilliant her magic friend was. She smiled proudly at the little puppy who was sitting nearby watching, visible only to her.

'Thank you, Robyn,' Krista's aunt said. 'It's very nice to meet you. I wish we had more time to talk, but now we must go.'

'Yes. We have many things to buy before we return to our home in the north,' said her uncle.

'Goodbye, Robyn,' Krista said with a warm smile. 'Enjoy your holiday.'

'Thanks, I will. Bye, Krista,' Robyn said.

She and Storm watched as the girl and her aunt and uncle left the shop. As they walked past the glass shop front, Krista paused to wave.

Robyn waved back, feeling a little sad that she had to leave so soon. 'Krista seemed really nice, didn't she?' she said to Storm. 'What a shame that we'll never see her again.'

'I liked her too,' Storm woofed.

'Come on, Storm. Let's go and find

Dad.' She'd gone right off the idea of buying any presents from this shop.

Chapter
SIX

The next day passed quickly. *Sea Princess* sailed along through ever more majestic fjords and Robyn and Storm stood on deck to watch the spectacular scenery passing by. When the ship docked at another coastal town they went ashore with her parents to explore.

Before boarding again, she found time to dash into a shop and buy her mum

some traditional hand-knitted gloves.
She also bought her dad a wallet and
got felt slippers for her gran and
gramps. 'Great. That's my present-buying
finished.' *Except for Storm*, she thought,
wondering how she was going to buy
him a present without him seeing.

Later on Robyn, Storm and her mum
and dad sat in a cafe near the harbour.

Robyn stirred the floating blob of
fresh cream into her mug of hot
chocolate and then took a big sip.
'Mmm. Gorgeous,' she murmured,
licking her lips.

Her dad grinned around a mouthful
of cream cake. 'I'm not sure the
chocolate moustache's a good look on
you!'

'Ha Ha! Very funny.' Robyn pulled a

face at him and wiped her mouth.

She scooped up a big fingerful of cream and slipped it inside her shoulder bag for Storm to lick. His warm little tongue flicked over her fingers and she hid a fond smile. She loved having Storm as her friend and sharing this wonderful holiday with him.

Robyn gazed out of the window as she nibbled a spice biscuit and found herself thinking about Krista.

Robyn had told her mum and dad

about the cardigan incident in the shop and described Krista and Jorun's lovely clothes. 'Your young friend is probably from a Sami background,' her mum guessed. 'I read in our travel guide that the Sami people used to be known as Lapps and once moved around with their herds of reindeer. A lot of them live a more settled life now.'

Robyn remembered that Krista's Aunt Jorun had said they were returning to their home in the north. She thought it must be amazing to live in a land of ice and snow, where it got so cold that even the sea froze.

Sea Princess docked at a small port the next morning and Robyn, Storm and her parents made their way to a smaller boat, which was waiting to take them to see a large glacier.

Passengers piled into the boat and lined the rails. Robyn looked down into the dark freezing water, which was so much closer to them on this small boat, and shivered. It looked very cold and very scary – she held on to the boat rail as it set off. On the way to the ice cap, the vast frozen expanse that stretched its arms down into a number of deep valleys, they sailed between islets and skerries.

Robyn was waiting excitedly for her first ever glimpse of a glacier.

'We should see it in a minute,' she whispered to Storm, who was in her shoulder bag.

Storm nodded.

Robyn was unprepared for the
amazing sight that met her eyes. The
frozen river, cutting through the huge
snow-capped mountains, ended in a
breathtaking wall of towering ice, which
was reflected in the sea.

'Oh my gosh!' Robyn's jaw dropped.
'That's awesome!'

Sounds of cracking, like pistol shots,

rang out in the still air and some of the
passengers looked worried. Storm
whimpered and Robyn glanced down
to where he sat with his front paws
looped over the bag. He was twitching
his ears nervously.

'That noise is just the sound of
boulders getting crunched under the
ice,' the guide explained to the worried
passengers.

'Did you hear what that man said? It's
nothing to be scared about,' Robyn
whispered reassuringly to Storm. But
when he continued to stare at the
glacier intently, she frowned. 'Storm?
Did you hear me?'

There was an extra loud *bang!* and
an ominous grinding sound – Storm's
entire fluffy white body tensed and his

hackles rose along his back. 'There is great danger!' he barked urgently, leaping down on to the deck.

Robyn felt a familiar warm prickling flow down her spine as big golden sparks bloomed in Storm's fluffy white fur and his ears sparked with electricity. Suddenly, the little boat shot forward in a dazzling burst of speed.

Robyn grabbed hold of the rail again and clung on for dear life.

Storm whimpered as his claws skittered across the deck and he slid towards the rail, about to fall overboard into the freezing bottomless sea.

Robyn acted without thinking. Still hanging on with one hand, she swooped down and reached out. For

one heart-stopping moment, she
thought she had lost him. But then her
fingers closed on the scruff of Storm's
neck. Yes! Robyn hauled the terrified
puppy to safety and tucked his
trembling little form safely back inside
her bag.

'Thank you for saving me, Robyn!'

Storm barked, looking up at her gratefully with his big blue eyes.

'I'm just glad you're OK,' she replied, trying to stay on her feet and steady her shoulder bag at the same time.

The other passengers were bracing themselves as best they could as the small boat suddenly zoomed back out to sea in a shower of golden sparkles before stopping abruptly near one of the small islets.

'Storm! What's going on?' Robyn asked in a shaky voice.

Suddenly, there was a thunderous cracking sound and massive slabs of ice parted from the glacier and dropped into the sea with a resounding *splash!* To everyone's horror, a huge tidal wave began rushing towards the boat.

Robyn felt the colour drain from her face as the wall of water bore down on them with the speed of an express train.

Storm calmly lifted both front paws and sent another fountain of sparks whooshing across the sea at the tidal wave, which immediately sank without a trace. The small boat rocked gently as normal-sized waves brushed harmlessly against its sides.

No one else could have seen Storm's magic and the stunned passengers all began speaking at once.

Robyn looked down fondly at her little friend. 'You were amazing, Storm! We could all have been really badly hurt and you nearly were. Thank you.'

Storm gave a little shake as every last

spark faded from his thick fur. 'I am
glad I was able to help.'

'Are you all right, love?' asked
Robyn's dad, putting his arm round her
shoulders. 'I'm a bit shaken up myself!'

'I'm fine now,' Robyn said.

Beside them, Robyn's mum
shuddered. 'I dread to think what would
have happened if we'd been right under

the glacier when that sheet of ice fell off! Thank goodness the captain had the presence of mind to put on a burst of speed.'

'Whoever was responsible for saving us was very brave, wasn't he?' Robyn said meaningfully, reaching one hand into her bag to stroke Storm's warm fur.

She felt so proud of her friend. It was just a shame that no one else would ever know how wonderful he was.

Chapter
SEVEN

Robyn stood on deck, bathed in the
night's moonlight, with Storm cuddled
in her arms inside her coat. She was
still a little nervous after saving Storm
the other day and was determined to
keep her little friend safe.

It had grown colder as *Sea Princess*
steamed further north and this was the
coldest weather Robyn had ever

experienced. The icy air prickled inside
her nose as she breathed in. It was a
strange sensation.

Storm's ears were pricked up and his
breath fogged in the air as he gazed up
at the millions of silver stars that
seemed so close you could reach out
and touch them.

'Brrr!' Robyn said, trying to hide a

shiver. She was thinking of going
inside to get warm, but the tiny puppy
was obviously having such a good time
that she didn't want to spoil his
enjoyment.

'You are cold, Robyn,' Storm noticed.
'I will make you warm.'

A familiar warm tickling sensation ran
down Robyn's backbone as tiny gold
sparks bloomed deep within his fluffy
white coat. Instantly, she felt a thick
layer of fur lining her jeans, her jacket
and even her hat and gloves, and she
was as warm as toast.

'Thanks, Storm, that's much better.
Oh, look!' Robyn breathed in wonder
as a shifting curtain of glowing greenish
lights appeared and began rippling
across the clear winter sky. 'Those must

be the Northern Lights. Aren't they amazing?'

'They are like the lights of my homeland. We often see them in the sky,' Storm woofed softly, sounding a little sad.

Robyn wondered what Storm's home world was like. Perhaps it was a land of ice and snow too. It must be a strange and wild place, where the great magical wolves that lived there fought over their lands. She felt a pang as she thought that Storm might be homesick and thinking of his wounded mother and the scattered Moon-claw pack.

Bowing her head, Robyn kissed the top of Storm's silky little head and held him close.

'Robyn? Is it really you?' called a voice.

Robyn almost jumped out of her skin. She spun round to see the slim dark-haired girl from the knitwear shop standing there with a broad smile on her face.

'Krista!' she said delightedly. 'What are you doing here?'

Krista smiled. She wore a red parka with a fur-trimmed hood. 'I am on my way back home, with my uncle and aunt. I did not realize that you were on a cruise round the coast. We use the coastal steamers, like *Sea Princess,* as local ferries to get around.'

Robyn remembered seeing that *Sea Princess* had a ferry and car deck. 'Where do you live? Is it very far

away?' she asked, hoping that there
might be time for her and Storm to get
to know Krista better.

Krista told her. 'We will reach the port
in two days, on Christmas Eve. My
village is a short distance inland. I live
there with my mother and father, my
brothers and sisters and aunts and uncles
and cousins and all the rest of my family.
I will be very glad to see them again.'

'You live with *all* of your family?'
Robyn asked curiously. She did get a
bit lonely with her dad away a lot of
the time, but Robyn wasn't sure she'd
want to live with a whole lot of other
people. 'Do you travel about a lot after
your reindeer herds? Sorry. I didn't
mean to sound nosy. I'm just interested,'
she said, blushing as she realized that
she seemed to be asking lots of
questions.

Krista laughed. 'That is all right. At
this time of the year, we live in houses,
but others, like my grandmother and
grandfather prefer to live in a *lavvo* –
that's a traditional tent,' she explained.
'Lots of other Sami families live in the
village too. We make things to sell,
until the season for calves to be born,

and then everyone helps out with the hard work.'

'Cool,' Robyn said, fascinated. Krista's life was completely different to her own. It sounded so busy and exciting.

Krista smiled at her enthusiasm and her slanted dark eyes twinkled. 'Would you and your parents like to visit my village and meet my family?'

'Would I? I'd love it!' Robyn said at once. 'But I'll have to ask my mum and dad if it's OK. They're in the main lounge. Why don't you come with me, then you can meet them?'

Krista nodded. 'I would like that. I will go and fetch Uncle Nikolai and Aunt Jorun. They would like to meet your parents too.'

As Robyn went below decks with

Krista, she whispered to Storm. 'Isn't it great that we've bumped into Krista again?'

Storm's little face lit up and he woofed in agreement.

Robyn woke the following morning, feeling full of excitement. Storm was curled in the crook of her arm. As she stirred, he opened one eye and then tucked his nose back between his paws.

'Come on, sleepy-head!' Robyn teased, gently tickling his furry little

sides. 'We're meeting Krista for breakfast.'

Storm stuck out all four fluffy white legs and had a big stretch before jumping to the floor.

Robyn threw back the quilt and got dressed quickly. Her parents were showered and ready and they all went to the restaurant together. Robyn spotted Krista at a table the moment she and Storm walked in. She waved to her as she helped herself from the usual display of delicious food.

'Hi,' Robyn said as she went and sat next to Krista.

'Hello, Robyn. Did you sleep well?'

'Yes, thanks. Oops,' Robyn said, as she felt Storm scrabbling up on to her lap. She pretended to drop her fork and just managed to stop him from slipping off again.

The adults joined them with their plates of food. Mr Parsons and Uncle Nikolai began chatting about football. Robyn's mum and Aunt Jorun talked about knitting, having discovered that they shared a passion for handicrafts the previous night.

'They all seem to be getting along very well, don't they?' Robyn commented to Krista.

'Yes, they do,' Krista said. 'I am very pleased that your parents have accepted my invitation to visit our village.'

'Me too. I can't wait,' Robyn said eagerly.

'I'm glad you said that,' Krista replied, her eyes glinting mysteriously. 'I have told my cousin Morten that you are coming to visit. He is arranging a surprise for you.'

Robyn smiled, wondering what it could be.

Chapter
EIGHT

Later that day, Robyn and Storm
were walking past some fishing boats
frozen into the ice on a village wharf,
on their way to meet up with her
mum and dad who were in the
supermarket opposite. Robyn couldn't
stop thinking about what Krista's
surprise might be. She smiled down at
Storm happily – this was turning out

to be one of her best Christmases
ever.

Suddenly, Robyn heard some furious
snapping and growling. It was coming
from a car parked outside a
supermarket. In the back were two
large dogs, who were scrabbling at the
window.

Storm whimpered in terror and
cowered against Robyn's legs. She could

feel him trembling from head to foot through her warm boots.

'Shadow knows where I am. He has sent those dogs to attack me,' Storm whined.

Robyn tensed as she saw the street lights gleaming on the dogs' pale eyes and extra large teeth. How was she going to save her little friend? She was just about to pick Storm up and run away as fast as her legs would carry her when a man came out of the supermarket and got into the car. The fierce growling and barking eventually faded as the car pulled away.

'Those horrible dogs have gone now. You're safe with me,' Robyn said. She picked Storm up and hurried into a narrow side street.

The tiny puppy pressed himself against her and looked up at her with fearful eyes. 'For now, perhaps, but Shadow will use his magic on other dogs we meet. If any of them find me, I may have to leave quickly, without saying goodbye.'

Robyn couldn't bear to think of losing Storm so suddenly. 'Maybe if we hide you really well, Shadow will give up looking for you and then you can stay with me forever. I'll take you home with me when the cruise ends. You'll love it there.'

Storm reached up and touched her face with one fluffy white front paw.

'That is not possible. One day, I must return to my homeland to lead the Moon-claw pack. Do you understand that, Robyn?' he barked, his little face serious.

Robyn swallowed hard, but she forced herself to nod as she went back towards the supermarket. She didn't want to think about anything, except enjoying every single moment of her Christmas holiday with Storm.

Christmas Eve finally arrived and Robyn and Storm stood beside Krista as *Sea Princess* steamed into the harbour with her horn blaring. The greyish winter light hung over the small town, which banked steeply up the hillside behind the harbour.

The ship was only staying for a few hours as the Christmas festivities would soon begin on board.

'Will it take long to get to where you
live?' Mrs Parsons asked Krista.

'Not long at all.' Krista looked at
Robyn and her lips curved in another
of her mysterious smiles.

Robyn was puzzled. What could
Krista be planning?

Ten minutes later, when she and
Storm were getting off the ship, Robyn
gave a cry of delight. A beautiful
wooden sleigh, pulled by two reindeer
in brightly coloured harnesses with
woollen tassels stood waiting.

'Wow! This is fantastic,' Robyn
enthused.

'What a wonderful surprise,' her dad
said.

Krista smiled. 'I thought you would
like it. This is Morten, my cousin,' she

said, introducing the tall young sleigh
driver.

'Pleased to meet you,' Robyn said,
smiling.

Robyn's mum and dad greeted him
and then Morten helped them climb
aboard the sleigh, before helping to load
the supplies.

Robyn settled Storm on her lap and
they nestled beneath the warmth of
the thick furs. Krista sat next to her.
Once everyone was settled, Morten
twitched the reins and the reindeer
sped off across the snow in a jingle of
sleigh bells.

'This reminds me of that "Winter
Wonderland" song!' Robyn's dad
said. 'In the lane, snow is glistening.
Can't you hear, logs are blistering . . .'

he began, singing all the wrong
words.

Robyn saw her mum give him one
of her looks and dig him in the ribs.

Robyn stifled a giggle as her dad fell
silent. Krista glanced at her mum and
they both fell about laughing.

Storm sat upright on Robyn's lap,
looking around at the thick blanket of
white snow. More flakes began to fall,
dancing in the glow of the sleigh
lanterns.

Soon lights were visible in the gloom
ahead. Robyn saw buildings with turf

poking up through the snow on their roofs. Tall cone-shaped tents were dotted about. She could smell woodsmoke on the frosty air.

As Morten brought the sleigh to a halt, people hurried out to welcome back Krista and her aunt and uncle. Robyn smiled and shook hands as she was introduced to Krista's parents, her brothers and sisters, and countless aunts and uncles and cousins. She knew she'd never remember all of their names.

'My grandparents would like to welcome you to their *lavvo*,' Krista explained. Robyn, Storm and the adults were shown inside one of the tents.

Colourful wall hangings and a crackling log fire inside the *lavvo* made it very warm and cosy. Delicious smells came from a metal cooking pot hanging over the flames. Robyn sat down close to the fire and Storm came and curled up beside her.

Krista's grandparents made them very welcome with food and hot drinks. Afterwards, a woman entertained them with traditional chanting and storytelling, while playing on a skin drum covered with drawings.

'We call this *joik*,' Krista told Robyn. 'Storytelling is an old tradition of my people.'

Storm sat up and pricked his ears, enjoying the entertainment. 'I like this place,' he woofed.

Robyn reached down to pat him, to show that she did too. But she didn't dare risk whispering to him with all the people around.

Krista showed Robyn round her house too. It was similar to the houses back home, with a modern TV and a computer, but there was a large wooden hut and a wooden pen for reindeer attached to the side of it. Krista's mum made fabulous jewellery with silver wire.

Time passed all too quickly and soon they had to return to *Sea Princess*.

There were many goodbyes and hugs all round. Morten drove the reindeer sleigh back to the harbour and Krista insisted on coming along with Robyn to keep her company.

As the sleigh drew to a halt at the harbour beside the huge bulk of *Sea*

Princess, Krista slipped something into
Robyn's hand.

'I made this. It is for you,' she said.

Robyn looked down to see that it
was a tiny reindeer horn carving of an
arctic wolf. The tiny wolf looked just
like Storm as his real self. It even had
chips of some glittery dark-blue
material for eyes.

'Oh, it's beautiful. Thank you,' she said
warmly, giving Krista a hug.

'I am glad that you like it,' Krista said, her tilted dark eyes moist.

'I love it to bits,' Robyn said with a catch in her voice. 'Goodbye, Krista. And thanks for letting me meet your family. I had the best time ever. I'll send you an email when I get back home.'

Krista's face brightened. 'Oh yes, please do. And maybe we can talk online. It will be wonderful to keep in touch with each other.'

'Definitely!' Robyn promised. She wished this Christmas could last forever.

Chapter
NINE

Robyn stood on board *Sea Princess*
with Storm in her arms. They were
looking down at the harbour, where
Morten was turning the sleigh around.
The reindeer and Krista, huddled in
the sleigh among the furs, looked
tiny now.

Krista waved one small mitten as the
reindeer plunged forward and the sleigh

moved smoothly away on wooden runners.

'Goodbye. Safe journey!' she called.

'Goodbye!' Robyn cried, waving.

She and Storm waited until they could no longer hear the sound of sleigh bells, before going inside the ship.

Robyn's mum walked beside her. 'Well, that was wonderful, wasn't it?

Krista's family were so hospitable. You must get me their address. I'd love to send them something from England when we get back.'

Robyn thought that was a great idea.

'Well, shall we go and see if anything's happening in the lounge yet? I fancy singing a few carols,' her dad said.

'Sounds great. I'll just be a minute. I want to get something from the cabin,' Robyn replied.

She was going to fetch the gloves and wallet, which were hidden at the end of her bunk. She wanted to wrap them and then sneak them under the enormous Christmas tree, so her mum and dad would be able to open them later.

Storm padded beside Robyn at her

heel as she went below decks. They had just stepped into the corridor leading to their cabin when Storm gave a yelp of terror and shot forward.

'What's wrong?' Robyn said, frowning.

Storm stood beside the cabin door, pawing frantically at it. She could see that he was trembling from head to foot.

Suddenly, Robyn heard fierce growling. Whipping round, she saw the shadows of two large dogs coming down the stairwell on the wall behind her.

Robyn's heart missed a beat. Shadow must have found Storm when they were on land and sent his dogs on to the ship after him! He was in terrible danger.

Robyn didn't think twice. She hurtled down the corridor and unlocked the cabin door with shaking fingers. She and Storm dashed inside, just as a fierce snapping and growling sounded right behind them.

'Oh!' Robyn shielded her eyes with her hand as a dazzling flash of bright light lit up the entire cabin.

Storm stood before her, a tiny fluffy white puppy no longer, but a majestic young silver-grey wolf. Hundreds of tiny diamond-bright lights glowed from his thick neck-ruff. Beside him stood a larger wolf with a gentle expression and large golden eyes.

And then Robyn knew that Storm was leaving for real.

She went forward and threw her arms

round the wolf's neck. 'I'll never forget
you, Storm,' she said.

Storm allowed her to hug him for a
moment and then gently pulled away.
'You have been a good friend, Robyn.
Be of strong heart,' he rumbled in a
deep velvety growl.

Robyn nodded, unable to speak as
she felt a tear run down her cheek. She
remembered that she hadn't been able

to get Storm a Christmas present. It seemed wrong not to give him something.

She had a sudden thought. 'Please, wait!' Reaching into her pocket, she took out Krista's gift. She held it out to Storm. 'This is for you. To remind you that, one day, you'll be a great leader of the Moon-claw pack,' she murmured.

Storm reached out and closed his huge paw over the tiny carved wolf. 'Thank you, Robyn. You are very kind.'

There was a final burst of intense gold light and a great shower of gold sparks exploded silently into the air and drifted harmlessly down around her. Storm and his mother faded and were gone.

The fierce growling outside the cabin stopped and silence fell.

Robyn felt a deep ache. She would never forget Storm, but she would always have her memories of the incredible Christmas holiday she had shared with the magic puppy.

The cabin door opened and her dad stood there. 'Oh, there you are, love. Are you coming up to the lounge? There's a carol service on and afterwards Father Christmas is going to give out presents.'

Robyn quickly dashed away a tear and smiled. 'Just coming!'

A Whole New World of Christmas Puppy Fun & Games!

Snowy Christmas Crossword

Magic puppy Storm loves finding out about Christmas in this world! How much do you know?

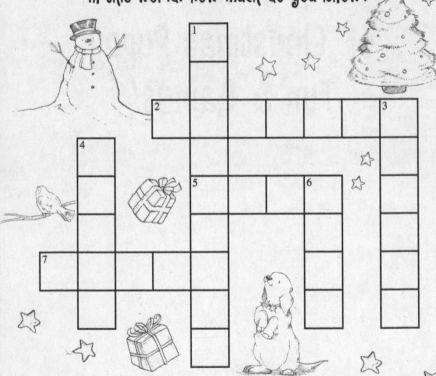

Across

2 Something that you get given at Christmas.

5 It falls out of the sky at winter and is fluffy, cold and white.

7 The name of a very special magic puppy!

Down

1 A very festive time of year.

3 You decorate a Christmas tree with this sparkly stuff.

4 He comes down the chimney at Christmas time.

6 What kind of creature is Storm in his own world?

Dot-to-dot

Join the dots to find a little magic friend.

16 15 14 13 12
17 11
18 19 10
20 1 9
21 2 3
22 8
23 57 7
4 56
6 5
24 55
25 54
26 53
34 47
27 33 35 52 48 46
32 49
28 31 37 36 51 50 45
29 30 38 39 41 42 43 44
40

Your Very Own
Christmas Tree

You will need: ★ Green card ★ Scissors (ask an adult to help you with this tricky bit) ★ Crayons, glitter or star stickers to decorate

★ Put two pieces of rectangle-shaped card together and fold them in half long-ways.

★ Draw half a Christmas tree opposite the fold.

★ Cut along the Christmas tree line so that you get two identical trees.

★ Cut a slit down the middle of the top half of one tree and up the bottom half of the other.

★ Slip the two trees together along the splits.

★ Decorate with crayons, glitter or stars to make your Christmas tree sparkle!

Puppy Trails

Can you find the trail of stars that
will lead Storm to his presents
under the Christmas tree?

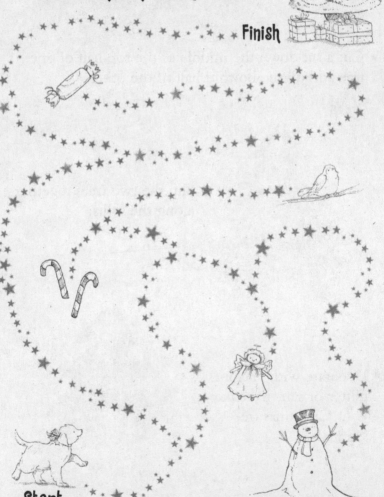

Finish

Start

Colour by Numbers

Use the key to colour in this festive Christmas scene.

Colour key:

1 green	**4** blue	**6** brown
2 red	**5** purple	**7** white
3 yellow		

Spot the Difference

Can you spot the eight differences between these pictures of Storm and Robyn's magical sleigh ride?

How Many Bones?

Brrr! The chilly weather has given Storm a big appetite. How many of his delicious bones can you spot in this picture?

Draw the Missing Half

Can you finish the picture of this Christmas tree? Add as many decorations as you like then colour it in.

Christmas Crackers!

Q: **Where** do snowmen go to dance?

A: A snow ball!

Q: **Why** is it always so cold at Christmas?

A: Because it's in **December!**

Q: What is Father Christmas's puppy called?

A: Santa Paws!

Q: What do Father Christmas's elves do after school?

A: Their gnome work!

Q: What happens when you eat Christmas decorations?

A: You get tinsel-itus!

Memory Test

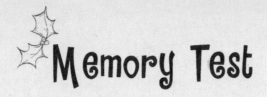

Look carefully at the picture, then cover
it up with a piece of paper.
How much can you remember?

1. There are three fairy dolls hanging on the wall.

True ☐   False ☐

2. There are two Christmas trees in the picture.

True ☐   False ☐

3. There is one little red robin outside the window.

True ☐   False ☐

4. Storm is looking out of the window.

True ☐   False ☐

5. There are three stars decorating the big Christmas tree.

True ☐   False ☐

6. All the presents are under the Christmas tree.

True ☐   False ☐

Answers

Snowy Christmas Crossword

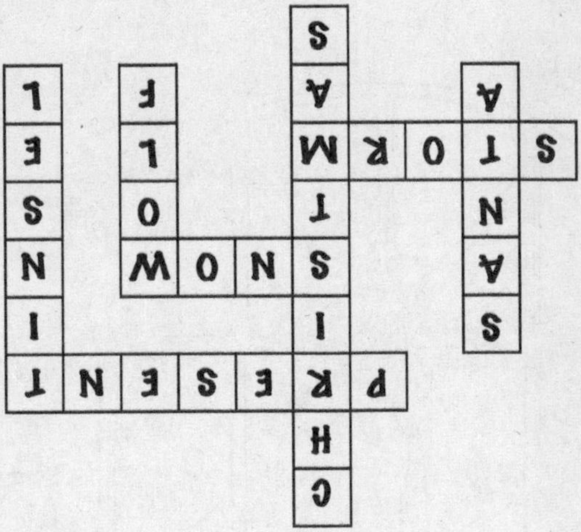

The crossword grid spells out:

- STORM (across)
- SANTAS (across)
- SNOW (across)
- PRESENT (across)
- FLOWF / F L O W (down)
- TINSEL (down)
- SANTAS (down)
- CHRISTMAS (down)

Puppy Trails

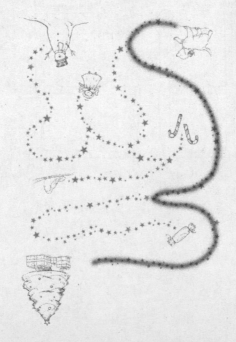

Spot the Difference

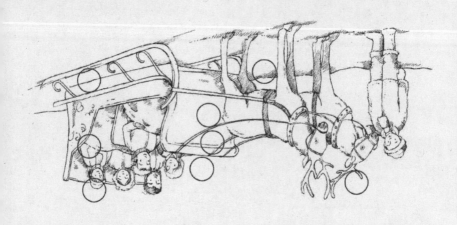

How Many Bones?

There are ten bones in the picture.

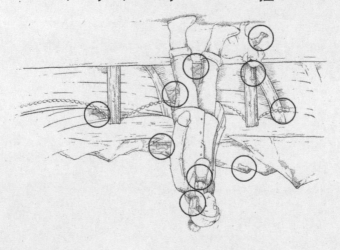

Memory Test

1.False 2.True 3.False 4.False 5.True 6.False

Win a Magic Puppy goody bag!

The evil wolf Shadow has ripped out part of Storm's
letter from his mother and hidden the words so that magic puppy
Storm can't find them.

Storm needs your help!

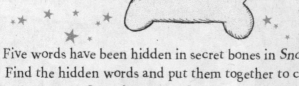

Five words have been hidden in secret bones in *Snowy Wishes*.
Find the hidden words and put them together to complete the
message from Storm's mother. Send it in to us and each month
we will put every correct message in a draw and pick out
one lucky winner, who will receive a Magic Puppy gift
– definitely worth barking about!

Send the hidden message, your name and address on a postcard to:
Magic Puppy Competition
Puffin Books
80 Strand
London WC2R 0RL
Good luck!

puffin.co.uk

★ A little puppy
a sprinkling of magic,
a forever friend

A New Beginning
9780141323503

Muddy Paws
9780141323510

Cloud Capers
9780141323527

Star of the Show
9780141323534

Party Dreams
9780141323794

A Forest C
9780141323

l of Mischief
0141323824

puffin.co.uk

Snowy Wishes
9780141323831

Classroom Princess
9780141324791

Friendship Forever
9780141324784